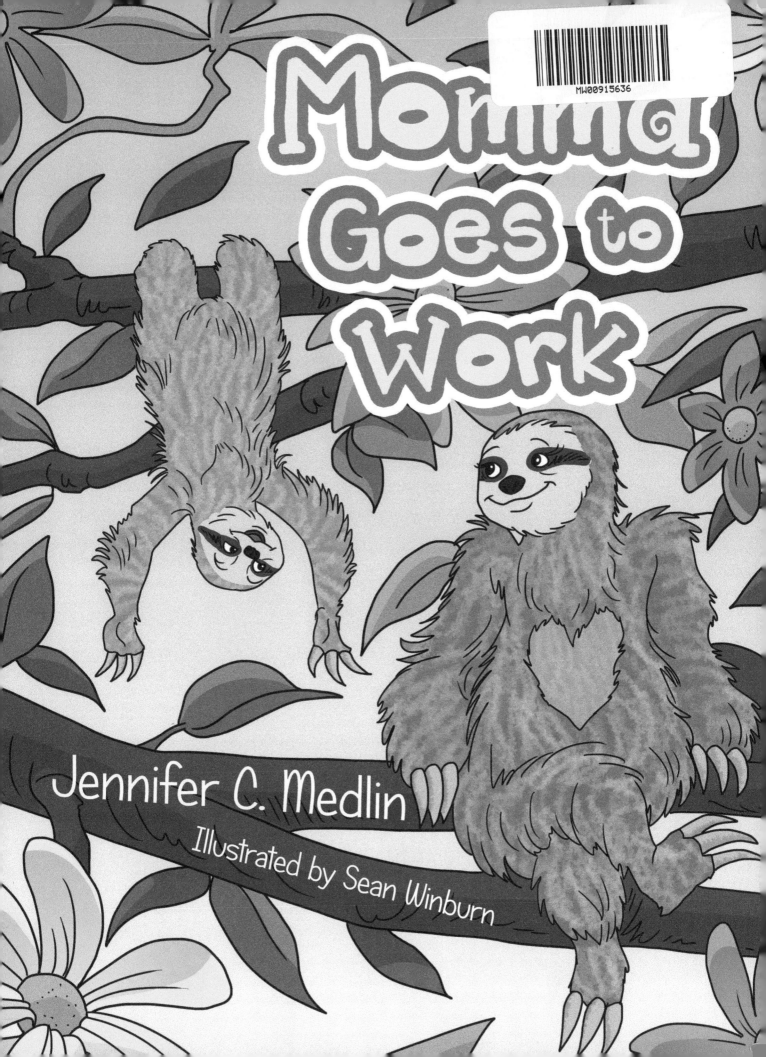

Momma Goes to Work

Jennifer C. Medlin

Illustrated by Sean Winburn

AuthorHouse™
1663 Liberty Drive
Bloomington, IN 47403
www.authorhouse.com
Phone: 1 (800) 839-8640

Because of the dynamic nature of the Internet, any web addresses or links contained in this book may have changed since publication and may no longer be valid. The views expressed in this work are solely those of the author and do not necessarily reflect the views of the publisher, and the publisher hereby disclaims any responsibility for them.

Any people depicted in stock imagery provided by Getty Images are models, and such images are being used for illustrative purposes only.
Certain stock imagery © Getty Images.

This book is printed on acid-free paper.

ISBN: 978-1-7283-4292-4 (sc)
ISBN: 978-1-7283-4293-1 (hc)
ISBN: 978-1-7283-4291-7 (e)

Print information available on the last page.

Published by AuthorHouse 01/15/2020

author**HOUSE**

Momma Goes to Work

To my amazing daughter.

Life as a working mother came with a lot of guilt about having to leave. I am a flight attendant. Even at her youngest, my daughter was always understanding and never used my absence as an excuse to not be her best self. She is an amazing soul.

To all the working moms out there. I hope this helps you and your children better understand that no matter where we are, mothers love their children and think of them always.

Momma goes to work.

Momma goes to work to make money to pay for the house and food and fun!

Momma chooses someone she trusts
to watch you while she's gone.

Sometimes it's a sitter, sometimes you're
at school, and sometimes it's a family
member who lets you break some rules.

Momma thinks of you when
she leaves to work.

Momma thinks of you when she eats lunch.

Momma thinks of you when
she's hard at work.

Momma misses you a bunch.

Momma thinks of you on her way home.

Momma is so happy when she
gets to see your face!

Momma wants a big, tight hug. She loves your warm embrace!

Momma wants to hear all about your day.
What did you do? What games did you play?

Momma asks you to help make dinner,
so she can teach you how to cook.

Sometimes you learn new recipes
by reading from a book.

Momma gave you an important job
to help clean up the mess.

Momma loves it when you pitch
in and finish all your tasks.

Momma wants to help you with
your homework because she
knows you are so smart!

Momma says it's time to brush
your teeth and turn off the TV. It's
time for sleep. Now march!

Momma reads you a bedtime
story and tucks you in tight!

Momma gives you a big kiss
and turns out the light.

You are always on Momma's mind
even when you are apart.

Momma goes to work and does
everything she does because she loves
you, and you are always in her heart.

CPSIA information can be obtained
at www.ICGtesting.com
Printed in the USA
LVHW071129200120
644161LV00021B/1010